Wet World

Felice Arena and Phil Kettle

illustrated by
Mitch Vane

First published in Great Britain by
RISING STARS UK LTD 2004
22 Grafton Street, London, W1S 4EX

Reprinted 2004, 2005, 2006

For information visit our website at:
www.risingstars-uk.com

British Library Cataloguing in Publication Data

A CIP record for this book is available from the British Library.

ISBN: 978-1-904591-78-8

First published in 2003 by
MACMILLAN EDUCATION AUSTRALIA PTY LTD
627 Chapel Street, South Yarra, Australia 3141

Associated companies and representatives throughout the world.

Visit our website at www.macmillan.com.au or
go directly to www.macmillanlibrary. com.au.

Project Management by Limelight Press Pty Ltd
Cover and text design by Lore Foye
Illustrations by Mitch Vane

Printed in China

Contents

Matt   Nick

CHAPTER 1

Wet Weekend

Matt and Nick are not only best mates at school. They live near to each other. On weekends these best friends like to be outside playing. Today is a really special Saturday for them. A new water slide has just opened in their area and they are very excited.

Matt "I can't wait for Wet World to open today."

Nick "Me neither. I heard that the water slide is mega."

Matt "I reckon people will come from everywhere to try out our water slide."

Nick "Yeah, and they'll be able to watch us and see how good we are."

Matt "I reckon we'll be so fast that people will want to take pictures of us."

Nick "We might get our pictures on posters all over the place."

Matt "There might even be buses driving down the street with pictures of you and me on the side of them."

Nick "If that happened, we'd be real legends at school."

CHAPTER 2

Get Ready!

Nick and Matt's mums have decided
to take the boys to the new water
slide and have packed a picnic
basket. It won't be long before the
boys are inside, ready to hit the water.

Matt "Wow ... look at the size of the water slide."

Nick "It must be the longest in the world."

Matt "How long do you think it is?"

Nick "Must be at least five kilometres."

Matt "It's got to be the biggest slide in the whole universe!"

Soon the boys are inside Wet World. Their mums make them put sunscreen on their faces and then watch as Matt and Nick run towards the first water slide.

CHAPTER 3

Get Set!

The boys stand at the bottom of the ladder that leads to the top of the water slide.

Matt "Gee, it's a long way up."

Nick "Yeah, that makes it a long way to the bottom when we get to the top."

Matt "How high do you think it is?"

Nick "I reckon it'd have to be as high as the biggest tree in the world."

Matt "I'll be going so fast on the way down that I'll break the sound barrier."

Nick "Well, I reckon I'll be going so fast that I'll make the water in the slide boil."

Matt "Yeah, right."

The boys climb to the landing, having decided to first go on the Sidewinder water slide, which is half way up, beside the main slide.

Nick "Will we go on the solo ride first?"

Matt "I'm sure I can go down a lot faster than you."

Nick "Lucky they time everyone as they come down. I wouldn't want you to tell any big ones."

Matt "Well, at least I can tell the time."

Nick "I wonder if you get a wedgie when you go down the slide?"

Matt "Only if your pants are too big!"

Nick "Well, let's go solo first then and see who's the best."

CHAPTER 4

Go!

Matt and Nick are waiting on the ramp for the Sidewinder. It is nearly their turn to go down. The attendant tells them that they are not allowed to stand up while they are going down the slide.

Nick "I'm going to lie on my back when I go down—I reckon I'll be going 1000 kilometres an hour!"

Matt "Well, I'm not going to try to break the world water slide record the first time. I'm just going to get faster every time I go down."

At last the boys have got to the
head of the queue and it's their turn.
They look down the slide. They can
see the pool of water at the bottom.
It looks a long way away.

Matt "Gee, this slide looks a lot
longer looking down it than when
I was standing on the ground
looking up."

Nick "Yeah, imagine what it's like
right at the top. So are you going
to go first?"

Matt "I thought you could go first."

Nick looks at Matt, then walks
to the slide. He sits down on the
take-off ramp. The attendant tells
him to push himself into the water
stream when he's ready.

Matt "Go on. Hurry up."

Nick starts to push himself into the water slide. He has a very serious look on his face.

Nick "Woweeeeee!"

Matt then gets into position, ready to push himself into the water slide. Nick disappears around a bend in the slide on his way to the pool at the bottom. Matt pushes off and starts his race to the bottom.

Matt· "Coooool!"

Splash! Then another *splash!* Nick, then Matt, lands at the bottom.

Matt "Wow, that was such cool fun."
Nick "Yeah, I really ripped. That was the fastest I've ever gone in my life."

Matt "I did a somersault when I left the slide."

Nick "I didn't see that. Maybe you just thought you did one."

Matt "You were still under the water when I did it."

Nick "Yeah, I was still underwater fighting a shark!"

Matt "Hurry up—let's do it again."

Nick "I wonder how we can go faster—faster than the speed of light."

Matt "Nah, just a bit slower than the speed of light or no-one'll be able to see us."

The boys head up to the slide and have another go. They splash into the pool at the bottom again.

Nick "I think I know how to make us go a lot faster."

Matt "So, what's your plan?"

Nick "Come on, let's get out of the pool. We have to get ready for our super run down the water slide."

CHAPTER 5

Speed Sliders

Matt and Nick get out of the pool
and run to where their mothers are
sitting and talking. Nick quietly
reaches into his mother's bag and
takes out the tube of sunscreen. He
starts to rub the sunscreen onto the
bottom of his swimming trunks, then
passes the tube to Matt.

Matt "What are ya doing? Why did you rub the sunscreen on the bottom of your trunks?"

Nick "It'll make us slip through the water and we'll be able to go a lot faster."

Matt "Great idea, but I hope we don't go so fast that we totally fly out of the water slide!"

Nick "We'll go on the two-person ride this time."

The boys make their way to the top of the water slide and get ready for the ride of their lives.

Matt "I want to go at the front."
Nick "Okay. If we're going so fast that we leave the water slide, you'll crash first and I'll land on top of you."

The attendant tells the boys that it
is their turn. They sit down, ready to
go, with Matt at the front. Nick
wraps his arms around Matt's waist.
They push off and start the long trip
to the bottom.

Matt "Hold on mate, here we go!"

Nick "I am holding on. We're going really fast."

Matt "I think I've left my stomach back at the start."

Nick "That's good. Now you can't puke all over me—I'd hate to have to clean it up!"

The boys splash into the bottom of the pool. They come out of the water laughing.

Nick "That was really good fun. Let's go again."

Matt "Yeah. I'm goin' to have some
food first so we can go on the
water slide all afternoon."

Nick "Cool, but don't eat too much
or you really will puke."

Matt "You never know—it might
work better than sunscreen!"

Nick "Agh, gross!"

Nick

BOYS RULE!
Water Slide Lingo

Matt

belly flop What happens when you come off the water slide and land in the pool on your stomach—ouch!

summer holidays A long break from school—the best time of year to go to places where there are water slides.

theme park A fun park where there are water slides and other fun activities.

wedgie When your trunks go down the water slide a lot slower than you do!

BOYS RULE!

Water Slide Must-dos

☞ Always go down the water slide as fast as you can.

☞ Try to race your best friend—it's always good to beat them too!

☞ Put sunscreen on the bottom of your swimming trunks—it will help you go faster.

☞ Try all the different sliding styles—on your back, on your stomach and on your bottom.

☞ Try to invent your own sliding style that no-one else has come up with.

☞ If you can't go to a theme park, then try to make your own water slide. Put some plastic on some soft ground outside. Then wet it and run and dive onto it to see how far you can slide.

☞ Eat plenty of food before you go on the water slide—the heavier you are, the faster you'll go.

☞ Wear your waterproof watch on the slide so you can time yourself.

Water Slide
Instant Info

 A water slide is like a wet roller coaster with no seats and no harnesses.

 You have to be taller than 110 centimetres to go on most water slides.

 The simplest form of water slide is a small, curved hill, made wet by a constant stream of water.

On many rides, you head into an "exit flume" at the end. This is a long channel of water that slows you down gradually.

 Wet 'n' Wild is the largest water park in the UK. It is situated near North Shields in the county of Tyne and Wear.

 There are often over 100 lifeguards on duty at a water park at any given time—better to be safe than sorry!

 Summit Plummet, in Florida is the tallest, fastest water slide in the world. You ride without a mat, zoom down and reach speeds of up to 60 miles an hour.

Think Tank

1 Should you wear sunscreen when you go out in the sun?

2 What is a wedgie?

3 Where is the Wet 'n' Wild theme park?

4 What shape would the fastest water slide in the world be?

5 Would you or your best mate be the best water slider in the world?

6 What goes down a water slide quicker—you or the water?

7 Do you have to always use a mat to go down a water slide?

8 Do you think that dogs should be allowed to go down water slides?

Answers

8 Only take your own dog on a water slide, if the attendant lets you.

7 No, but it usually helps you go faster.

6 You go down the water slide quicker than the water.

5 You, of course!

4 The fastest water slide in the wrold would go straight down!

3 Wet 'n' Wild is near North Shields in the county of Tyne and Wear.

2 A wedgie is when your pants slide up your butt too far.

1 Yes, always.

How did you score?

- If you got all 8 answers correct, then think about going to a theme park and having a go on a water slide.

- If you got 6 answers correct, you should probably only go in the swimming pool.

- If you got only 4 answers correct, it might be safer to just get your best mate to turn the hose on you in the backyard.

Felice →   ← Phil

Hi Guys!

We have loads of fun reading and want you to, too. We both believe that being a good reader is really important and so cool.

Try out our suggestions to help you have fun as you read.

At school, why don't you use "Wet World" as a play and you and your friends can be the actors. Set the scene for your play. Find some props such as swimming trunks and sunscreen and use your imagination to pretend you are at your favourite theme park, about to hit the water slide.

So ... have you decided who is going to be Matt and who is going to be Nick? Now, with your friends, read and act out our story in front of the class.

We have a lot of fun when we go to schools and read our stories. After we finish the kids all clap really loudly. When you've finished your play your classmates will do the same. Just remember to look out of the window—there might be a talent scout from a television station watching you!

Reading at home is really important and a lot of fun as well.

Take our books home and get someone in your family to read them with you. Maybe they can take on a part in the story.

Remember, reading is a whole lot of fun.

So, as the frog in the local pond would say, Read-it!

And remember, Boys Rule!

BOYS RULE!

When We Were Kids

Felice

Phil

Phil "Did you ever go on a water slide as a kid?"

Felice "Yeah, kind-of. I made my own water slide."

Phil "How did you do that?"

Felice "I put a long plastic strip on the ground and hosed it down. I took a long run up, then dived, and skidded on my stomach along the plastic."

Phil "That sounds like good fun. But how did you stop?"

Felice "I couldn't, but thankfully my sister was always standing in the way so I'd just run into her."

Phil "So sisters *are* useful."

What a Laugh!

Q What does a frog drink when he is at Wet World?

A Diet Croak.

BOYS RULE!

Gone Fishing

The Tree House

Golf Legends

Camping Out

Bike Daredevils

Water Rats

Skateboard
Dudes

Tennis Ace

Basketball
Buddies

Secret Agent
Heroes

Wet World

Rock Star

Pirate Attack

Olympic
Champions

Race Car
Dreamers

Hit the Beach

Rotten
School Day

Halloween
Gotcha!

Battle of the
Games

On the Farm